Flash's Special Lunch

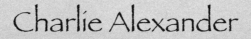

Charlie Alexander

Flash's Special Lunch

By Charlie Alexander

Flash's Special Lunch

Written by Charlie Alexander

Art Work by Charlie Alexander

Flash was so happy to meet Suzy and Mitch!

Some friendships are very important!

Mitch asked Rasdog to drive.

Flash was a little jealous!

Fat Tiki was painted on the side of Mitch's truck.

What a great name for a mobile restaurant!

Mitch needed more fresh fruit.

Yummy!

Rasdog liked showing Flash the ropes!

He was very friendly to Flash.

Flash wanted to know what was on the menu.

It was easier to help folks that way.

The Turkey was cooked to perfection.

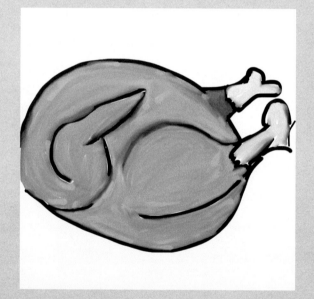

It smelled like heaven!

Most people were happy to pay!

All the meals were very special.

Filling the bucket with soap and water.

It was time to clean the pots and pans.

It was fun to help!

Flash didn't even mind all of the scrubbing.

Flash carried the big
green barrel.

He was strong enough to carry it by
himself. But he was glad to have help.

Rasdog asked Flash to
sweep the area.

Sweep, Sweep and Sweep again.
Flash liked making things look nice!

Suzy was ready to bake a
pumpkin pie.

Fresh orange pumpkins are so
good!

The line of people was
very long!

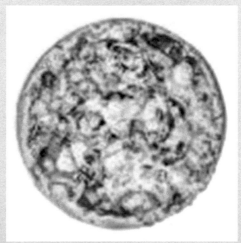

The aroma of the delicious Pizza
was calling them.

Someone ordered a cold glass of lemonade.

Flash delivered it with a smile.

Flash was learning a lot from Rasdog!

It was fun to have a chance to be a team!

He was shopping for more vegetables.

Flash knew exactly what Mitch needed!

Flash loved cooking on the grill.

He hoped Mitch would ask him to prepare some hamburgers!

Rasdog and Flash each
wanted the same hamburger.

It was big enough for both of them!

French fries sure hit the spot.
"I have to watch my weight!" Flash exclaimed.

Hot and crispy. It was just the way
Flash enjoyed them!

Fish was on the menu.

Mitch knew how to make a wonderful lunch with a secret way of cooking fish.

The truck arrived right on time.

The new spot looked busy!

Working inside the truck was so cool.

Rasdog and Flash worked well together!

Flash and Mitch took a little rest.

They both worked very hard all afternoon!

Flash thought the picnic area should be mopped.

He just had to find the mop!

Flash used some fresh water
so the lawn would stay green.

It hadn't rained in days!

Flash went to get the water hose.

He wanted to refresh some beautiful flowers.

Flash looked for the mop for a few minutes.

He finally found it!

"I sure do like ice cream!"

said Flash.

Especially three scoops!

The work day is finished.

It's time to head home!

Flash was very tired.

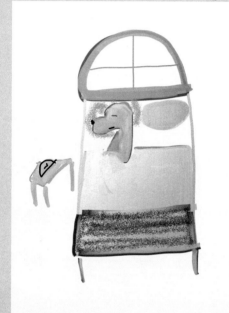

He went to sleep right away!
The End

Flash has a special Lunch! He learned so much about helping Mitch ,Suzy and Rasdog. Flash washed lots of pots and pans. He also washed sinks full of dishes and glasses and cups. He even enjoyed mopping the floor. Flash enjoyed his french fries and of course his ice cream cone!

Charlie enjoys making children smile as they read his books. He lives in Ocala Fl. With his wife Becky and his pal Flash!

To order additional copies of this book, contact:
Xlibris
844-714-8691
www.Xlibris.com
Orders@Xlibris.com

Library of Congress Control Number: 2023902625

ISBN: 978-1-6698-6707-4 (sc)
ISBN: 978-1-6698-6708-1 (hc)
ISBN: 978-1-6698-6706-7 (e)

Print information available on the last page

Rev. date: 04/13/2023

Printed in the United States
by Baker & Taylor Publisher Services